D1195330

The Hunted
Polar Prey

Sara Louise Kras

Speeding Star

To Hayden Jarvis, my nephew and first reader

Speeding Star, an imprint of Enslow Publishers, Inc.

Library of Congress Cataloging-in-Publication Data:

Kras, Sara Louise.
    The hunted : polar prey / Sara Louise Kras.
        pages cm
    Summary: "Jeremy must save his mother who is stranded on an iceberg in the Arctic
while being hunted by a polar bear. But when the only person who can save her hasn't flown a
helicopter in years, Jeremy is left with a lot of doubt"—Provided by publisher.
    ISBN 978-1-62285-080-8
    [1. Survival—Fiction. 2. Rescues—Fiction. 3. Polar bear—Fiction. 4. Bears—Fiction.
5. Arctic regions—Fiction.] I. Title.
    PZ7.K8648Hu 2014
    [Fic]—dc23   2013031227

Future editions:
Paperback ISBN: 978-1-62285-081-5
EPUB ISBN: 978-1-62285-082-2

Single-User PDF ISBN: 978-1-62285-083-9
Multi-User PDF ISBN: 978-1-62285-158-4

Printed in the United States of America
112013 Bang Printing, Brainerd, Minn.
10 9 8 7 6 5 4 3 2 1

To Our Readers: We have done our best to make sure all Internet addresses in this book were
active and appropriate when we went to press. However, the author and the Publisher have no
control over, and assume no liability for, the material available on those Internet sites or on other
Web sites they may link to. Any comments or suggestions can be sent by e-mail to comments@
speedingstar.com or to the address below.

Enslow Publishers, Inc., is committed to printing our books on recycled paper. The paper in
every book contains 10% to 30% post-consumer waste (PCW). The cover board on the outside
of each book contains 100% PCW. Our goal is to do our part to help young people and the
environment too!

Speeding Star
Box 398, 40 Industrial Road
Berkeley Heights, NJ 07922
USA
www.speedingstar.com

Cover Illustration: iStock/© thinkstock.com

Contents

Chapter 1

Frozen Sea

Polar Bear

Way up north in the Arctic on the Hudson Bay, a huge polar bear lay quietly on the frozen sea. In front of him was a small hole. He raised his nose and sniffed. Below him under the thick ice, he could smell seal. The seal swam in the freezing arctic waters. The polar bear knew it was only a matter of time. The seal would need air.

The bear laid patiently by the hole all day. First it heard bubbles. The polar bear crouched next to the hole. Then a furry head popped out. The bear quickly swung at the seal with its huge paw. But the seal was too quick. Its head popped back down below the watery surface. Angry, the bear pounded the ground again and again. He was getting weaker from lack of food.

Chapter 2

Stuck on an Iceberg

Jeremy

Several miles south of the polar bear stood three buildings. A snow-covered sign hung on one of them. It read, "Global Warming Research Station." This was a place where scientists studied the affects of global warming in the Arctic. Inside one of the buildings, a satellite phone rang. "Hello," said Jeremy as he clicked it on.

"Jeremy! The ice floor cracked. I'm floating on an iceberg. My phone battery is low. Write this location down."

Jeremy's jaw tightened. He recognized the voice. It was his mom's.

Mom was in trouble, floating somewhere in the Arctic.

Nervously, Jeremy dug for a piece of paper.

This was bad, very bad, he thought. Ice breaking off from the mainland had become more common with global warming. This incredibly dangerous situation could kill anyone nearby. He had heard of people disappearing forever into the Arctic sea.

He grabbed a pen. "Go ahead, Mom."

"My location is 59 north, 50 minutes, 20 seconds latitude and 95 west, 10 minutes, 15 seconds longitude. This position will change. Is your father back yet?" The phone crackled.

"No, Mom. Dad's still gone."

"All right. Try to call him. Also, make a note. I'm slowly headed in a northeastern direction."

"OK. I'll get on it."

"Quick, Jeremy, quick! I've got to go. I'll call in about an hour." Then she hung up.

"Mom! Mom!" There was no response. With shaking hands, Jeremy put the phone down. His chest knotted as a horrible feeling washed over him.

This is serious. Mom could die, he thought. I don't have much time. Why did Dad have to fly down to Churchill today to get supplies? Why did Mom have to go out to get ice samples?

Jeremy could feel tears well up in his eyes. He quickly wiped them away.

This didn't seem fair. He was too young to have to deal with this. But deep inside he knew it didn't matter that he was only twelve years old. It was up to him to save his mom. And that's just what he planned on doing.

Quickly, he dialed his dad's number. "Hello. This is Tom. Please leave a message."

Jeremy moaned. He left a message and hung up.

Dad won't be back for several hours. I can't wait for him. I have to do something now. What can I do? How can I save my mom? thought Jeremy.

Chapter 3

Crack!

Paula

After calling the research station, Paula, Jeremy's mom, turned off her phone to save the battery. She looked across the crack. The gape was too large to jump. Her snowmobile was parked only about twenty feet away. But Paula couldn't reach it. The edge of the iceberg reached far down into freezing cold water. She watched as she slowly floated away from the mainland. Then she quickly gathered all her bags and equipment. The iceberg will be thickest in the middle, she thought. So she dragged everything there.

Once she was done, she looked around. The iceberg measured about ninety feet long—the size of a basketball court. Its blue color gleamed in the sun as it slowly drifted.

All of a sudden a loud rumbling noise filled the air. The iceberg bumped hard into a large chunk of ice. Paula heard high-pitched screeching then a sharp sawing sound. CRACK! The ground shook beneath Paula, causing her to fall. A chunk of the iceberg crashed into the sea. Paula groaned. I hope Jeremy gets help to me fast. I don't know how much longer this iceberg is going to last.

Chapter 4

The Plan

Jeremy

Jeremy tried to form a plan. But he didn't have much to work with. There were only two other crew at the station.

I know Dad has one helicopter, but is the other one here? thought Jeremy. He knew the station usually had two helicopters. The helicopters transported supplies. Sometimes they moved roaming polar bears that got too close to the station.

I know the other pilot has flown home to Winnipeg. But did he take the helicopter with him?

Jeremy wasn't sure. He had to find out. Maybe the helicopter could help save his mom.

Jeremy ran back to his tiny bedroom. He pulled off his sheepskin slippers and jogging pants. He slipped into two pairs of long johns. Then he put on thick ski pants. He pulled a heavy sweater over his head. On his feet were wool socks and rubber boots. He pulled a ski mask over his face. After putting on his green-hooded jacket, he pulled his down gloves on and headed outside. The cold air stung like needles on his lips.

He jogged over to the hangar and pulled the door back. Inside sat a helicopter.

Whew! OK. The helicopter can be used to rescue Mom. But how can I fly the helicopter? I don't know how. Think, Jeremy, think! Every minute I waste is putting Mom in more danger. If the cold doesn't kill her, the wildlife could.

Jeremy remembered a story about a man hunted by killer whales. He was on an iceberg. One of the whales jumped out of the water. It hit the iceberg, making it tilt. The man started sliding towards the sharp-toothed whale. The remaining killer whales surrounded the iceberg. Jeremy couldn't remember how or if the man lived.

Maybe the other crew can help me, he thought.

He closed the hangar door and ran back to the living building. Inside in the kitchen he found George, the cook. George stirred something in a large bowl. Penny, an assistant, sat at a table hunched over a book. He told them about his mom.

"Gosh. What should we do? Should we get on the snowmobiles and see if we can find her?" asked George as he set the bowl down on the counter.

"But that won't help. She's floating in the sea."

"You have a point," said George.

"What about the helicopter?" inquired Penny.

"That's what I thought. Do either of you know how to fly it?"

Penny and George looked at Jeremy with a blank stare.

There's got to be someone who can fly that helicopter. But who? he thought.

That's when he remembered. About a year ago Felix, his friend, had told him his dad used to fly helicopters. But then he had a terrible crash. After the crash Felix's dad never flew again.

"I'm going to the Inuit village," blurted Jeremy.

"Why?" asked George.

"Maybe Felix's dad can help save my mom."

Chapter 5

Webbed Paws

Polar Bear

The polar bear pushed through the icy water with his webbed front paws. His muscles tightened as his back legs lay flat to steer. A thick layer of blubber kept him warm and helped him float. Only his head and upper back were above the water's surface. He had been swimming for over an hour. Small scattered icebergs floated away as he swam. Hunger drove him on. Seal had become harder and harder to find.

Off in the distance, a loud cracking noise filled the air. Then the water swelled up and came down. The polar bear raised his black nose high and sniffed. A smell of fresh meat hit his nostrils. It wasn't seal, but it was meat. It was coming from the left—the location of the noise. He turned towards its direction and continued further out to sea. The smell of fresh meat pushed him forward.

Chapter 6

Inuit Village

Jeremy

Jeremy grabbed the keys to the snowmobile and went outside. The wind bit into his exposed eyes and lips. He put goggles on that looked like a snorkeling mask. After hopping on a snowmobile, he turned it on. It roared to life. Jeremy took off towards the Inuit village.

In all directions Jeremy saw snow-covered ground. He pulled the throttle all the way back. The snowmobile let out a loud hum as it flew over the icy surface. Jeremy looked ahead. He thought he saw something move. With a jerk he released the throttle and then stood up. There! He saw it again. He stared hard at the spot. It moved again. It was a ball of fluffy white fur with a long tail. It bounded across the snowy ground, chasing something. That's when Jeremy realized what it was. It was nothing but a snow fox. He let out a sigh of relief. It was mid-November and polar bears were everywhere. Jeremy continued to look. He knew a snow fox sometimes followed a polar bear. Snow foxes were known to pick at the leftovers from a polar bear kill.

Jeremy looked for a couple more minutes. Nothing else moved. He sat back down and pulled on the throttle. The snowmobile let out a loud whine. The noise often scared wandering polar bears. But if a polar bear was hungry enough, it could attack.

Jeremy usually loved riding the snowmobile. He'd been driving one ever since he was ten. That's when he arrived at the research station. Since then two years had passed. But, right now he didn't love driving. All he could see were pictures of his mom cold, alone, and in the middle of the huge Arctic sea.

Will she make it? Can I save her? he thought.

He'd remembered his mom's advice. Advice she told him after he'd panicked in a blizzard. The strong wind and heavy snowfall had made everything white. While walking between the supply building and the living building, Jeremy lost his hold on the connecting rope. Because he could hardly see his hand in front of his face, he became lost within minutes. His mother sensed something was wrong. She went out to find him. He was wandering only a few feet away from the building walls. She grabbed him and pulled him inside.

Once inside he shivered for about fifteen minutes. His mother wrapped him in warm blankets. Then she gave him hot chocolate. After he'd calmed down, she looked him in the eye. "Never panic again. This is life and death stuff. The Arctic is an unforgiving place. You need to stay calm. Life can sometimes be scary. The way to beat it is to be clever. Fix the problem. My father told me that when I was a young girl. It's kept me alive facing some very scary problems. Probably, more times than you'll ever know."

Would Mom remember her own advice? thought Jeremy.

Off in the distance, he saw smoke curl. Gray buildings blended in with the snow. He had reached the Inuit village.

Chapter 7

Sea Ice

Felix

Inside one of the homes in the Inuit village, Felix heard the hum. He knew it was a snowmobile. Why was it coming to the village? He put on his down jacket. Then he slipped his feet into his heavy winter boots. Pulling his jacket tight, he walked outside. The cold air stung his nostrils. The white sky hung above him. Dark clouds formed in the distance. He knew these signs. Another snowstorm is coming, he thought.

He peered toward the oncoming noise. The snowmobile got closer. He recognized

Jeremy's green coat. Felix waved his arms. The snowmobile began to slow. It drifted to a stop close to him. Felix could see that Jeremy looked worried.

"Where's your dad?" Jeremy asked. "I need to see him right away."

"He's over at my uncle's. Why?"

"My mom. She's in danger. I need your dad to fly the helicopter."

Felix sucked in the cold air. It made his teeth hurt.

His father had not flown since the accident.

"What happened to your mom?" asked Felix.

"The ice cracked. She's drifting. If we don't act quick, we might not find her!"

"You're right. This is not good," said Felix. He had been taught the power of the tuvaq, or sea ice, before he could walk. The tuvaq was so strong, when it moved, it could crush a large ship. But the constant swirling sea beneath the tuvaq sometimes weakened it. When this happened, huge pieces would crash into the sea.

Three years ago, his father had saved him from the tuvaq. Felix had been nine years old. He and his father had been fishing for many days. While packing up, Felix heard loud thunder and looked up into the sky. His father grabbed him by the arm. Then he ran, dragging Felix along the ground. The ice where Felix had been standing had disappeared. It had plunged into the sea. Freezing water splashed up over the remaining rim of ice.

Just last year one of the tribesmen had been killed by the tuvaq. He had gone out alone to hunt seal. He never returned. Felix's father went in search of the man. He found his snowmobile along with some of his gear.

It stood next to a sheet of ice which had been broken. Men in the village quickly gathered. Canoes with motors were pushed into the water. Searching went on for the rest of the week. No one was found.

"My dad is on the other side of the village," said Felix.

"Get on. I'll drive over there," said Jeremy.

Chapter 8

Helicopter Crash

Felix

Felix hopped on the back of the snowmobile and pointed the way.

Once they arrived, they went inside. Felix found his father and uncle sitting at the kitchen table. Two cups of coffee steamed in front of them. They murmured in conversation. A long scar ran across his father's cheek, a reminder of the helicopter crash.

The crash had happened when Felix was young. Felix's mother told him that his father had been caught in a blizzard. The helicopter spun out of control. It crashed to the ground.

All Felix remembered was his father was gone for many months. When his father came home, he looked very ill. His skin was gray. His eyes were dull. Felix tried to talk to him. But his father had nothing to say. It was as if his father was gone.

Felix's mother called the village shaman. Felix heard them talking from the other room. "There is an evil spirit," said the shaman, "He haunts your husband. What we must do is change his name."

"But his name, Pujjuut, ought to be respected. It was given to him by a dream," said his mother.

"Yes, it will be," said the shaman, "But his name still must be changed. This will confuse the evil spirit that harms your husband. The evil spirit will search for Pujjuut, but he will not find him. Please bring your husband to me tomorrow."

When Felix's father returned two days later, his name was Johnny. It was the first time Felix saw his father smile after the accident. Even so, Felix's father couldn't work. Instead, he received aid from the government. Felix knew his father was ashamed. It was as if the helicopter crash still held a horrible curse over his father.

Will my father be willing to help Jeremy's mother? thought Felix.

"Excuse me, Father," Felix said quietly to show respect.

His father looked up at him.

"Jeremy's mother is in danger. He has come to ask for your help."

Felix's father looked over at Jeremy.

"Mr. Tugak, I'm sorry to disturb you." Jeremy quickly told about his mother's phone message.

"This is very serious," said Felix's father. "What can I do?"

"There's a helicopter at the base. Felix told me you used to fly."

Felix saw a dark shadow pass his father's face.

"But I haven't flown a helicopter in over five years."

"Please Mr. Tugak. My dad is in Churchill. There's no one else."

Felix held his breath while his father stared at the wall for several seconds.

"Yes, I will try," Felix's father whispered.

Chapter 9

Cold Arctic Wind

Paula

Paula carefully walked around the edges of the iceberg. She saw no more signs of cracking. It looks like it might hold, she thought. Close to one edge was a tall rounded hill. She climbed on top of it. She could see the mainland. It was just a speck in the distance now. She crossed her arms and rubbed her shoulders. Chills ran through her body. I'm getting cold. I need to get warm and soon, she thought.

Water sloshed against the sides of the iceberg. Cold arctic wind blew in her face. The sea surrounded her, dotted with smaller icebergs. What if Jeremy can't get help? How long will I be out here? Even if someone finds me will I be alive? The satellite phone is almost drained. I've got no food. I've got no protection. Her heart beat hard against her chest. She knew she was beginning to panic.

Paula closed her eyes. Slowly, she began to breathe in and out, in and out. You need to remain calm, she thought. What is the most important problem to fix?

Protection. I need to keep warm. The wind will kill me.

Ridges were scattered across the iceberg. One ridge was near the center facing against the wind. It stood about four feet tall.

This is a good start for protection. I'll make a pit to shelter me from the wind, she thought.

Quickly Paula got to work. She went through her equipment. In it she found a pick and small shovel. She began to dig a hole next to the ridge. A bead of sweat ran down her cheek while she worked. That's when she saw it. Something moved off in the horizon. Paula got out her binoculars and ran up the small hill. A white head bobbed. Strong furry arms pushed it through the water. It was a polar bear and it was headed right toward her iceberg.

Chapter 10

Running Out of Time

Jeremy

Jeremy watched as Felix and his dad got onto their snowmobiles. He jumped onto his and followed them. The white landscape blurred past. He was running out of time. It was around 2:00 p.m. The sun would be down in less than three hours. He could feel the clock ticking inside his head.

Mom can't survive long in the cold. I've already wasted almost an hour coming to the village.

Jeremy had the throttle pulled all the way back. It seemed as though it took forever as they made their way to the station.

Finally, after driving over a small hill, he could see the buildings. Felix and his dad had just pulled up. Jeremy curved in beside them. "The helicopter is in the hangar," said Jeremy, "We need to push it out."

"I have to do a safety check first," said Mr. Tugak.

"OK. I'll go get the key and the satellite phone."

A burst of warm air hit Jeremy in the face as he entered the building. The key to the helicopter was in his dad's drawer. Then Jeremy picked up the satellite phone. He dialed his mom. The phone rang and rang. Mom, pick up, he thought. He paced the small room. The phone continued to ring. After twenty rings, it clicked off.

Mom, hold on. We're coming! He wanted to yell.

Chapter 11

Hunger

Polar Bear

The polar bear could sense it was getting closer to the smell. He saw something move on top of the iceberg. His hunger pushed him faster through the water. During the long summer months, the polar bear had nothing to eat. It had begun hunting in late October. But he had only been able to catch one seal. He needed more blubber to keep strong and warm. The polar bear's instincts kicked in. His stomach squeezed. His muscles strained. Finally, he would have more food.

Chapter 12

There's a Polar Bear!

Paula

Paula sank to the ground. She knew she was dead. Polar bears were fierce hunters and they were always hungry. Almost nothing could stop them. Remain calm, she thought, remain calm. What do I need to do first? Contact Jeremy. Give him my new location. Then get something to defend myself. She knew all she had was a small rifle in her pack.

Paula jumped up and ran over to her satellite phone. After switching it on, she called Jeremy.

"Mom, where are you?" asked Jeremy.

Paula breathed a sigh of relief. Just hearing Jeremy's voice made her feel a bit better. "My new position is 60 north, 15 minutes, 35 seconds latitude and 96 west, 30 minutes, 20 seconds longitude."

"Got it, Mom. We're on our way. We should be there in about ten minutes."

Ten minutes. Does that give me enough time? Paula looked across the water. The polar bear was about a half-mile away. "Jeremy," she yelled, "There's a polar bear!"

"Mom!" Jeremy called. Then the phone went dead.

Paula threw the phone onto the ground. She ran over and pulled her rifle out of her backpack. All I can do now is wait, she thought.

Chapter 13

Frozen

///

Felix

Felix and his dad walked into the hangar. The helicopter was covered with a canvas cloth. After pulling off the cover, his dad said, "We need clean rags."

Felix searched and found a bucket of rags on the floor. "We will check these fluids." His dad pointed at different fluid dipsticks in the engine. They quickly got busy. Felix noticed his dad's hands were shaking.

"Everything looks good for take off," said Felix's dad, "Let's push it out."

They struggled as they pushed the helicopter out onto the snowy ground. Jeremy ran toward the helicopter. He was carrying a large rifle.

"Why do you have the rifle?" asked Felix.

"My mom just called. A polar bear is headed toward her iceberg. We have to go now before it's too late!"

Felix sucked in his breath. Nanuk, the polar bear, is hunting. This is not good. Nothing can stop Nanuk, except for bull walrus, and even they lose sometimes. Last winter Felix saw a polar bear and walrus bull fighting on an iceberg. The walrus speared the polar bear with his three-inch tusks. But the polar bear continued the attack. The bear tried to bite through the walrus' thick skin. The walrus quickly slid into the sea and swam away.

"Did your mother tell you the size of the iceberg?" asked Felix's dad.

"She said it was small, but what does it matter. We need to leave now!" cried Jeremy.

Felix grabbed Jeremy's arm to try to calm him. He could tell the American was scared.

"We need to attach a carry bag to the helicopter. Do you know if the station has one?" asked Felix's dad.

"Yes. We have one in the hangar. It's used to carry supplies. But why do we need it?"

"The iceberg may not hold the weight of the helicopter. If I land, it might crack. Then all of us would die. To get your mother off the iceberg, she may need to get into the bag."

"I'll show you where it's at," said Jeremy.

Felix helped Jeremy get the large canvas bag from the shelf. They pulled it next to the helicopter. After they laid it out, it formed a square. A thick metal ring hung from each corner. Jeremy then pulled out a long metal cord. "This is hooked to the bottom of the helicopter. Then the bag is hooked on the end. Help me pull these rings to the hook," said Jeremy. After the bag was attached, Felix helped Jeremy pull it to the side.

"Make sure it won't tangle when we take off," said Felix's dad.

"We've fixed it, Father," said Felix.

They climbed into the helicopter. "Here's the key, Mr. Tugak," said Jeremy. He then reached over to the global positioning system (GPS) and punched in his mom's position. "My mom just gave me this location, but it might change," he said.

Felix sat back in his seat and clipped on the seatbelt. He waited for his dad to flip the switches. Silence. Nothing was happening. He looked over at his dad. It was as if he had frozen.

Chapter 14

The Curse

Felix

"Father," said Felix softly, "Jeremy's mother is being hunted by Nanuk. We must get to her quickly."

"I don't know if I can do this," his father whispered.

"Please, Mr. Tugak. My mother!" cried Jeremy.

Felix turned around and looked at Jeremy. "Shhhhhhhhhh."

Felix remembered how his mother helped his father after the accident. Even after his name changed, his father sometimes looked almost dead. Felix had always thought of it as the curse.

Felix knew it was important to be calm and quiet. "The evil spirit of the crash is not here with us," said Felix softly, "Your name is Johnny. The evil spirit cannot find you." Felix reached over and squeezed his father's arm.

"You can do this, Father. I know you can," he whispered.

Felix's dad took a deep breath and looked over at Felix. "You're right, son."

Nervously he began flipping switches on. The whine of the engine filled the helicopter. Within a couple of minutes they began to hover. The helicopter began swaying back and forth. Felix's dad struggled to steady the helicopter's throttle. The wind blew. Snow swirled, making it difficult to see.

Felix held tightly to the handle on the door. He could feel the blood drain out of his hand. Would he be in a helicopter crash along with his father and Jeremy?

What would happen to Jeremy's mother? They kept swaying back and forth as they climbed higher. Then the helicopter jolted once the bag beneath them flew into the air. Felix felt his stomach flip. I feel like I'm going to throw up, he thought.

They climbed higher and higher. The swaying got less and less until it stopped. Felix's stomach began to settle. He looked over at his father. A firm look was on his father's face as he pointed the helicopter toward the settings displayed on the GPS.

Chapter 15

Chunks of Ice

Jeremy

Jeremy watched as the white landscape flew by below him. He could see on the GPS they were closing the gap to his mom's position. On his lap the rifle was heavy. He checked it one more time to make sure it was loaded.

He remembered the first time he'd shot a rifle. His dad had taken him shooting when he was only eight. That was when they lived in California. A can of baked beans was set on a large barrel. A heavy rifle jammed against Jeremy's shoulder. Then he pulled the trigger. The rifle pushed him backward and he fell on his butt. But he hit the target. The can of beans exploded into the air.

But the rifle he held today was different. It didn't have bullets, only cracker shells. These types of shells sounded like firecrackers and were used to scare polar bears away, not harm them.

"We're almost there," said Felix as he pointed to the GPS.

Jeremy strained to look below. Nothing. Small chunks of ice looking like Styrofoam bobbing in the open sea. But then off in the distance to his left, there was a larger iceberg. "There!" he yelled as he pointed, "I think Mom's over there!"

Chapter 16

Fear

Paula

Thump, thump, thump. Paula heard the helicopter before she saw it. She began to cry and shake for joy. She had given up. But now there was hope. She grabbed her backpack and jumped up and down. The helicopter was just a small speck in the sky coming toward her. But then it swung off in the wrong direction.

"No!" she screamed, "I'm over here." Her heart sank. She knew the location she'd given Jeremy was no longer exact. The iceberg had been floating. She might be impossible to spot.

Where was the polar bear? Paula climbed the mound. This time she didn't need to use her binoculars. The polar bear was twenty feet from the iceberg. It was swimming fast. Fear shivered up her spine. She found it hard to breathe, like the air had been knocked out of her. I have to put distance between me and the bear, she thought. She ran down the mound to the other end of the iceberg.

That's when she heard. The helicopter was getting louder and louder. It was coming in her direction. Paula jumped up and down. "Here! Here! I'm right here!" The helicopter buzzed towards her. She was spotted. Paula looked at the other end of the iceberg. The polar bear had just appeared. It shook its fur, ridding it of excess water. The polar bear then sniffed the air and began walking toward her. As it got closer, its head lowered and its ears flattened. Then, it let out a loud snort. Paula was familiar with polar bear behavior. She was being hunted.

Chapter 17

Bang!

Jeremy

Jeremy saw his mother jumping up and down on the iceberg. He felt such joy and relief. That's when Felix tapped his shoulder. "Look," said Felix as he pointed, "Nanuk is here."

The size of the bear was shocking. Even on all four legs, it was almost as tall as his mom. It inched its way towards her. Mr. Tugak pointed the helicopter at the bear and pushed down on the throttle. They swooped down. The bear crouched and began backing away.

Jeremy put the rifle on his shoulder and pointed it out the window. "Shoot the ground around the bear to scare it," yelled Felix, "You want to frighten it not make it angry." Jeremy shook his head to show he understood. It was hard to aim. The helicopter wasn't very steady. Jeremy squinted and looked through the scope.

Bang! The rifle kicked back intensely against Jeremy's shoulder. The cracker shell exploded into the air. The bear began running and then slipped over the iceberg edge. "Yes!" exclaimed Jeremy.

"Can we land to get my mom?" asked Jeremy.

"No," said Mr. Tugak, "The iceberg is too small. We'll have to use the carry bag. Tell me when she can reach it."

Jeremy stuck his head out the window and looked down. Wind from the propeller blasted cold air around his face. The helicopter went lower and lower. Finally, the bag rested on the iceberg. Jeremy tried to yell, "Get in, Mom!" But he knew she couldn't hear him over the loud helicopter. Even so, his mother started gathering her things and throwing them into the bag.

"The polar bear!" yelled Felix. Jeremy looked out the other side of the helicopter. The polar bear had reappeared. It began running straight for his mom. Jeremy opened the window and screamed "Mom! The polar bear! Get into the bag now!" He saw his mom look over toward the running polar bear. She dove into the bag. "Go! Go! Go!" yelled Jeremy. He looked down. His mom's eyes were big. She looked scared and small in the big bag. Jeremy put the rifle out the window. But the swaying of the helicopter made it difficult to aim. He pulled the trigger. Bang! The cracker shell exploded up in the sky too far from the bear. That's when he saw the polar bear charge and jump into the air. Its claws were stretched out toward the carry bag.

Chapter 18

Is Mom OK?

Jeremy

Jeremy strained as he looked below. He was trying to see inside the bag. But it was closed up tight. Is Mom OK? Did the polar bear claw her? He watched as they left the iceberg. The polar bear lay on the ground. His mom wasn't on the iceberg. She must still be in the bag. But is she injured?

Jeremy reached into his pocket and pulled out the location his mother had first given him. He punched it into the GPS. It was only about a mile away. "Mr. Tugak," he said, "This is where the ice first cracked.

My mom's snowmobile is here. Can we fly there?"

Mr. Tugak shook his head and pointed the helicopter in the direction.

On the way there Jeremy kept poking his head out the window. He saw movement in the bag. "Hang on, Mom! We're almost there!" he wanted to yell.

Up ahead, he saw where the ice had cracked off. His mom's snowmobile and equipment sat about fifteen feet from the water's edge.

I'm so glad Mom didn't fall into the water, he thought. There is no way she would've survived.

Just the thought of it brought shivers up his back.

Once over the mainland, the helicopter hovered. It slowly got lower and lower.

"Tell me when the bag is on the ground and where it is," said Mr. Tugak, "I don't want to land on it."

Snow swirled in the air from the whirling helicopter blade, making it hard to see. Both Jeremy and Felix stuck their heads out. The bag lay on the ground. "It's on the left," said Felix. Jeremy watched the bag. Nothing was happening. He stuck his head in. "She's not moving. She must be hurt," Jeremy yelled.

Chapter 19

Helicopter Landing

Jeremy

The minute the helicopter landed, Jeremy jumped out of it. Felix was right behind him. Jeremy and Felix tugged at the large rings attached to the bag. They each took a corner and pulled it back. Jeremy's mother curled up inside.

"Mom! Are you OK?" Jeremy yelled. He could tell his mom was trying to say something, but then she burst into tears. Jeremy scrambled over to her and hugged her. Her shoulders shook as she sobbed. After a few minutes she started to calm down. She pulled back and looked at him with tear-filled eyes. "I thought I was going to die. But now I'm safe. You saved my life, Jeremy!"

She squeezed him hard, and Jeremy squeezed her back. He noticed that her lips were almost blue. "You must be freezing, Mom. Let's get you in the helicopter."

Jeremy pulled her up. Her legs were shaking. Felix went to the other side and put his arm around her waist. Together, they helped her into the helicopter. Mr. Tugak put a blanket over her shoulders. Then he strapped her into the seat. "I should get her back to the station. We need to get her warmed up."

Jeremy nodded his head. "I'll drive Mom's snowmobile back. I'll see you there."

Jeremy loaded his mom's equipment onto her snowmobile. Then he got on, pulled the throttle back, and headed home. He could feel himself start to relax. The nervousness of the last few hours began to drain away. He looked around. The sunlight twinkled and flashed on the white snow. It's like another planet, he thought, nothing like California. He thought of his friends. He still e-mailed them back in the United States. The longer he was in the Arctic, the less he felt he had anything in common with them. They talked to him about video games, playing baseball, and the latest MTV hits. Yeah, it was fun keeping in touch. Jeremy had checked some of the stuff out on the Internet.

Even so, he knew his California friends would never understand what happened today. He'd done things they could and would never do.

How could I explain how it felt to save my mom from a polar bear? Would any of them understand what it was like to scare a bear away? Would any of them know how to use a GPS? Somehow, I don't think so.

Today was terrible. I don't want to have to do anything like this again, he thought.

But deep in his heart Jeremy was pleased. He now knew he could depend on himself when things went wrong.

Yes, I'm only twelve years old, but I sure know how to kick some butt! he thought.

Chapter 20

Proud

Felix

The helicopter flew smoothly through the air. After about ten minutes, the research station appeared. They began to hover as they slowly came down to the ground. Felix looked over at his dad. His dad's jaw was fixed. But he looked calm. His hand rested steadily on the throttle stick.

Father acts as though he's been flying his entire life, thought Felix.

Once they landed Mr. Tugak glanced at Felix and gave a slight nod.

He's proud. It looks like the curse of the accident has finally vanished, Felix thought. Felix had a huge smile as he helped Jeremy's mother out of the helicopter.

Chapter 21

Instinct

Polar Bear

The polar bear lay flat on the ice. His body was hot and he needed to cool down. After about a half an hour, he stood up. He was thirsty so he scooped up snow and licked it off his paw. After he rested he slipped back into the water. He headed north. The ice was slow in forming this year. Instinct told him seal were north. The polar bear had to get food soon or else he could die.

Author's Note

This story was based on a true story. The real story was about three scientists in the Arctic above Norway. They had shipwrecked on an island. The scientists were wet and had no weapons. Polar bears started to close in on them. After fifteen hours of being on the island, they were saved by a rescue helicopter.

I changed this story to take place in Manitoba, Canada, along the Hudson Bay north of the small arctic town called Churchill. This is where one of the largest groups of polar bears in the world gathers. The months of October and November are the best time to see them. They come to Churchill to wait for the ice to form on Hudson Bay. There are many scientists in the area studying polar bears and global warming.

I visited Churchill in November 2008. While there I saw about twenty-five polar bears. To view the polar bears the tourists travel in a Tundra Buggy. These huge buses have wheels that are six-feet tall.

Even though polar bears are dangerous, they can be funny to watch. Curious polar bears sniffed the air to try to identify the Tundra Buggy. One stood up on its back legs and tried to look inside. One slid down a snowy mound like a slide. Another sat on its bottom like a person and looked around. My favorite was a polar bear which rolled around and then lay on its back. It lifted its paw and licked the snow off of it.

If you like polar bears as much as I do and would like to find out more about them, go to http://www.polarbearsinternational.org/.